The Interdimensional Fish Sticks

by Aaron Starmer
illustrated by Courtney La Forest

Penguin Workshop

To Dave, Pete, and Magela—AS

For Kate, Phylicia, Sydney, and
Jeremy, for keeping me sane
through this crazier-than-
interdimensional-travel
last year. ily!! <3—CLF

PENGUIN WORKSHOP
An Imprint of Penguin Random House LLC, New York

The publisher does not have any control over and does not assume any
responsibility for author or third-party websites or their content.

Photo credits: page 190 (cube) enra/iStock/Getty Images,
page 191 (milk crate) greyj/iStock/Getty Images

Text copyright © 2021 by Aaron Starmer. Illustrations copyright © 2021 by
Penguin Random House LLC. All rights reserved. Published by Penguin Workshop, an
imprint of Penguin Random House LLC, New York. PENGUIN and PENGUIN WORKSHOP
are trademarks of Penguin Books Ltd, and the W colophon is a registered trademark of
Penguin Random House LLC. Manufactured in China.

Visit us online at www.penguinrandomhouse.com.

Library of Congress Cataloging-in-Publication Data is available upon request.

ISBN 9780593222898 (pbk)   10 9 8 7 6 5 4 3 2 1
ISBN 9780593222317 (hc)   10 9 8 7 6 5 4 3 2 1

Chapter One

A GREEN
SKITTLE

Bryce Dodd was in a pickle.

Well, not literally *in* a pickle. That would be salty. And wet. Being in a pickle was simply another way of saying that Bryce had a problem. Only he was refusing to acknowledge that problem at the moment.

He was too busy standing in front of his bathroom mirror, smearing green face paint on his skin, and singing a song. It was an original song by his favorite band, the Screamin' Beagles, and it was called "Weird New Place." The first verse went like this:

You know you are my favorite girl,
You send me to a different world.
Whenever I look at your face
I'm swept away to a weird new place.

He sang so loud that he almost didn't hear his mom calling out, "The bus will be here in five minutes! And Dad and I are leaving in four! Get moving!"

Five minutes later, Bryce was moving. Or perhaps *waddling* is a better description. He was waddling because of the green cardboard sphere wrapped around his body. The sphere had a white *S* marked on the front and green suspenders holding it in place. He also wore a green beanie, a green shirt, green gloves, and green pants. In other words, Bryce was dressed as a green Skittle.

"Uh-oh, Bryce," the bus driver, Mary-Ann, said as he squeezed on board. "Did you not hear the announcement last week?"

"The one about wombat poop?" Bryce asked. "And how scientists figured out why it's cube-shaped?"

"Um . . . no," Mary-Ann said. "The one from the vice principal. About the rules?"

She didn't need to tell him what the announcement was. The other kids on the bus were the only reminder he needed.

Today was Halloween. And Bryce was the only one wearing a costume. Because wearing a costume to school, even on Halloween, was against the rules.

Keisha James, a girl who lived her life by the rules, was sitting near the back of the bus, in the hump seat. Seeing Bryce all alone, and all in green, made her face go red. She had never been so embarrassed for someone. She hid her face in her hands.

Bryce noticed this, of course. It gave him a lump in his green throat. He had honestly thought that an overachiever like Keisha would be impressed by the effort he put into his costume. But she couldn't even look at it.

Hunter Barnes, a boy who spent his

life breaking rules, was sitting in the hump seat next to Keisha. His reaction to Bryce was the opposite. He couldn't stop looking at the costume. He hopped up, stood on the hump, and pointed a finger. Even though he was small, it made him tower over all his peers as he said, "Ha ha, this stinky Skittle doesn't know we're not supposed to dress up for Halloween! He's so busted!"

"Do you have another set of clothes?" Mary-Ann whispered to Bryce.

He shook his head. Most of the time Bryce wore a pair of shorts under his pants in case the weather got warm. But not today.

"Sorry, but I can't hold the bus and wait for you to get changed," Mary-Ann told him. "But if you want to go home and get a ride—"

Bryce shook his head again. His house was locked and his parents' car had already pulled away. The bus was his only option.

He had to go to school dressed as a green Skittle.

Chapter Two

VICE PRINCIPAL MEEHAN

Vice Principal Meehan stood on the front steps of Hopewell Elementary, next to a NO SKATEBOARDING sign. There was a large crate of apples at his feet, and he waved to students as they got off their buses. "Happy Halloween!" he called out. "There's enough sweet, delicious treats for everyone. Take one. Take two. Happy Halloween!"

Kids grabbed apples, mostly to be polite, as they walked into school. Meehan flashed them a thumbs-up and said, "Make sure to brush your teeth after."

But his cheery demeanor changed when Bryce lumbered up the steps.

"Oh no, Mr. Dodd," he said. "Oh no no no no."

"Yeah," Bryce replied with a sigh. "Costumes aren't allowed today, huh?"

"And yet you're wearing one," Meehan said, and he motioned to the door. "Come with me, son."

A few minutes later, Bryce was trying to sit in a chair in front of Meehan's desk, but his costume was too wide to fit between the armrests.

"You do know why we don't wear costumes to school, even on Halloween, right?" Meehan asked.

Bryce gave up his attempt to sit and stood like a giant green sun at the center of a solar system of books and office supplies.

"Because someone might mistake me for a real Skittle and try to eat me?" Bryce asked.

"No, Mr. Dodd," Vice Principal Meehan said with a hand on his head. "It's because they're a distraction."

"Okay. That makes a little more sense."

"I will be contacting your parents

about this, because the rules were clearly communicated. But first things first, you will remove the Skittle and wash your face."

Bryce wanted to explain that costumes were one of the ways he expressed himself. He wanted to tell Vice Principal Meehan that Halloween was the most important holiday of the year to him, because it was a celebration of being different. But that's not what Bryce said, because he wasn't sure he could say that without getting in trouble. Instead, he mumbled, "Yessir."

This satisfied Vice Principal Meehan, who replied, "I'll inform Mrs. Shen that you'll be missing homeroom. Now go clean yourself up."

"Yessir," Bryce said again. "But are there . . . more?"

"I assume you mean more consequences?"

Bryce nodded.

"Depends on if you prove to me that you're finally paying attention, Mr. Dodd. For now, go do as I asked."

Chapter Three

THE CRACKED MIRROR

Bryce stood alone in the basement bathroom known as the Dungeon. Fourth-graders sometimes used this bathroom as a secret meeting spot, because they knew no one else would ever step foot in it. The Dungeon was an awful place, a simply horrible bathroom. "Stinky, rusty, dark, and dusty," was the way Bryce often referred to it.

There were creepy squeaks and creaks. There was graffiti everywhere, including a message on one of the toilet stalls that read: *Flush The Toilet + U Will B Sucked into the Burrito Dimension!* But it was quiet and it was private and, by some miracle, the sink actually worked. Bryce could wash off his green face paint without anyone asking him why he broke the rules.

This was important, because Bryce didn't want to lie. He also didn't want to tell the truth.

The truth was this: He knew wearing a costume was against the rules at Hopewell Elementary, even on Halloween. He had known that ever since kindergarten, and he was now in fourth grade. Yet he did it, anyway.

This wasn't Bryce's way of rebelling, exactly. Instead, it could be explained by Bryce's very specific brain.

If you saw Bryce's brain, you would see a bundle of nerves and wrinkles and brain goo, just like anyone's brain. But if you saw the way Bryce's brain actually worked, you would see his thoughts were organized into two colorful, overflowing wicker baskets . . . and a drab plastic container with a lid sealing the top. The first colorful basket was spilling over with weird thoughts, while the second was jam-packed with nice thoughts. The drab plastic container, however, was where Bryce stored the thoughts that he preferred not to think about.

An example of a weird thought was one Bryce had recently. He wondered to himself if tornadoes could wear tuxedos. He was possibly the first person to ever wonder such a thing.

An example of a nice thought was pretty much any thought he had about Keisha. She was incredibly smart and brave and honorable. And he wanted nothing more than to be her friend.

An example of a thought he preferred

not to think about was knowing that wearing a costume was against the rules and knowing that it would get him in trouble. He had stored that thought far away from his other thoughts, as if it were leftovers pushed to the back of the fridge.

But now he had no choice but to pull those leftovers out, open them up, and smell their rotten smell. That's right. He had to accept that if he didn't ditch the cardboard and wash off the face paint, he'd face some serious consequences.

He turned on the tap and the water came out a dark brown. The mirror above the sink was cracked, and Bryce stared at the fractured reflection of his green face. He took a deep breath and said, "Here we go."

Then he turned off the tap and turned away from the mirror.

He walked out of the Dungeon, still green, still round, still looking exactly like a Skittle.

He headed toward Locker 37.

Chapter Four
LOCKER 37

Locker 37 was the universe's most wondrous creation, and it was conveniently located in Bryce's school. You probably don't have the universe's most wondrous creation in your school, because you probably don't go to Hopewell Elementary. And even if you do go to Hopewell Elementary, there's still a good chance you don't know about Locker 37.

When Bryce went to Hopewell Elementary, only the fourth-graders knew about Locker 37. They didn't share their secret with younger kids, and older kids forgot about the secret as soon as they finished fourth grade. The secret was that Locker 37 gave out magical objects and those magical objects could solve any problem.

Imagine if everyone in the world knew such a secret. There'd be a line down the hall from Locker 37, out the building, along the street, through the next town, into the next state, across the border to Canada, then into the Arctic Ocean, and down to the ocean floor. Even if you could provide enough food, shelter, and bathrooms for people in line, just think of all the scuba gear and wetsuits you'd need to supply. It would be entirely unsustainable.

Therefore, Locker 37 restricted its access to a few dozen fourth-graders every year. When Bryce approached it on Halloween morning, there was no line. He was alone in the dark hallway. Maybe no one else had a problem that needed solving that day. At least not yet.

Bryce would've preferred not to rely on Locker 37. He could usually figure out creative solutions to his problems. But he wasn't even sure what his problem was. He only knew that he wanted to wear his costume without getting in trouble. But what could help with that?

When he opened Locker 37, he got his answer. He smelled them before he saw them, but he could hardly believe his nose.

They couldn't be . . .

They shouldn't be . . .

And yet there they were, surrounded by an orange glow . . .

On a round plate, next to a dab of ketchup . . .

A pile of . . .

Freshly fried . . .

Fish sticks.

That's right. Fish sticks.

Chapter Five

YUCK, YUCK, YUCKETY-YUCK

"No way, no how," Bryce said as he looked at the fish sticks. "Yuck, yuck, yuckety-yuck."

He said this to no one in particular. Because no one else was there. Not even someone sneaking up behind him to interject some witty or surprising dialogue.

That meant no one was there to see whatever he decided to do next.

Would he get rid of the fish sticks? Because that's what he wanted to do. He wanted to throw them in a dumpster. Or better yet, he wanted to erase their existence from the face of the earth.

Was that even allowed? The items that Locker 37 gave out were extremely powerful things, such as:

- A gym pinny that would turn any fourth-grader who wore it into a professional level athlete . . . and the only ten-year-old in the world who could dunk a basketball.
- A pair of rain boots that made the wearer invincible. Walk through fire, dive into

a bottomless pit, eat really spicy chicken wings. As long as you were wearing these yellow rubber boots, you'd be fine.

- A tube of glue that could fix anything that was broken, including bones, school buses, and promises.

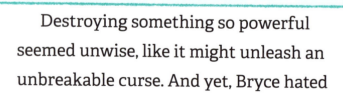

Destroying something so powerful seemed unwise, like it might unleash an unbreakable curse. And yet, Bryce hated the taste of fish sticks. He certainly didn't want to eat them.

But that's what he had to do if he wanted to solve his problem. It was obvious, especially since one word was written on the plate:

EAT

"Oh, come on, plate," Bryce said. "Be reasonable. Can't I do something else to the fish sticks? Like launch them into space? Or throw them into a pit of hot lava or something? "

But the word on the plate stayed the same.

EAT

"Fine, but just a nibble."

Bryce pinched his nose with one hand and lifted one of the fish sticks with the

other. With his front teeth he broke off the tiniest bit of fish stick, then gulped it down.

Not terrible. Though also not wonderful. But it was done.

"Now what?" Bryce said.

Well . . . this:

His eyes went blurry for a second. Or was it that the entire world went blurry? Bryce wasn't sure. But when the focus came back, he thought to himself, *Uh-oh, did I just come down with a turbocharged case of food poisoning?*

His stomach felt okay. He wasn't dizzy. Nothing seemed to have changed, except for that brief blurry moment.

Maybe the fish sticks hadn't worked.

Still, he knew it was probably best to hold onto them. Luckily, the plate could be hidden and balanced inside his costume on the ridges of the cardboard frame. Unluckily, he'd have to smell the fish sticks until he knew what to do next.

"Looking good, Bryce," a voice said.

This time there *was* someone sneaking up behind him, but when Bryce turned around to see who it might be, he couldn't be more surprised.

It was Vice Principal Meehan. And he was dressed as a pirate. Red coat with gold buttons, black hat, pantaloons, eye patch, even a parrot on his shoulder. A real live parrot!

"Looking good, Bryce," the parrot parroted.

"Whoa," Bryce said. "When did you put on a costume?"

Meehan's face twisted up in confusion. "What costume? This is how I always dress."

"How I always dress," the parrot parroted.

Bryce knew this wasn't true. He also knew that a few minutes ago, Meehan was wearing completely different clothes and was mad at Bryce for wearing a costume.

In other words, the fish sticks had . . . changed Vice Principal Meehan?

Yes. But Vice Principal Meehan wasn't the only one who had changed.

Chapter Six

HALLOWHAT?

Bryce hurried to music class without paying much attention to his surroundings. When he got there, he discovered that everyone was wearing costumes. Notorious mischief-maker Riley Zimmerman was dressed as a mad scientist, and that certainly fit with her wild hair. The klutzy Carson Cooper was dressed as a vampire, which was clever because it made all the stains on his shirt look like blood stains.

And, of course, the magnificent Keisha James was dressed as an astronaut with Olympic medals around her neck. Because why settle on dedicating your life to space exploration when you can dominate the world of international gymnastics as well?

Even the music teacher wore a costume. Mr. Gregson was dressed as a beagle, which made sense because he was in a local band called the Screamin' Beagles. In case you already forgot, the Screamin' Beagles were Bryce's favorite band. (But you wouldn't forget that because your memory is flawless.)

It was finally clear that eating the

fish sticks had changed things so that Halloween costumes were now okay to wear at Hopewell Elementary.

In other words: Bryce's problem was solved.

In other *word*: Hooray!

"Happy Halloween, my fine costumed friends," Bryce said cheerfully to the class.

And immediately the class fell silent.

"What did you say?" Mr. Gregson growled. Or did he scream? It was somewhere between the two, and entirely appropriate for a Screamin' Beagle.

"Happy Halloween!" Bryce hollered, so that everyone could hear him.

They did hear him, and they didn't like it. Everyone's faces changed. They suddenly looked . . . mean.

One of Keisha's hands shot up and she pointed at Bryce. "He said the forbidden words. The forbidden words!"

"Children," Mr. Gregson growled, and this was definitely a growl. "Eat him alive!"

All at once, his classmates started chanting, "Forbidden! Forbidden! Forbidden!"

All at once, they raised their hands and curled their fingers like claws.

And all at once, they started moving toward Bryce, a mob of costumed and angry fourth-graders.

Instinct took over. Bryce rushed for the exit.

For a moment, his Skittle costume was caught in the doorway, and he thought he might not make it to the hall. But it popped through a second before Keisha's hand lunged at him.

He had escaped.

Chapter Seven

BACK TO THE DUNGEON

"Yikes, yikes, yikedy-yikes!" Bryce cried as he waddle-sprinted down the hall, careful to keep the plate of fish sticks balanced inside his green cardboard sphere.

The only response he heard was the chant of "Forbidden! Forbidden! Forbidden!"

As the mob closed in, Bryce started

noticing differences in the school.

In place of janitor closets, there were vending machines, and the trash cans overflowed with candy wrappers.

In the classrooms, there were bowls of chocolate on each desk, and the whiteboards were projecting pictures of lollipops.

A poster on the wall read: DID YOU EAT YOUR GUMMY BEARS TODAY?

Everyone was now obsessed with candy. Though, apparently, they also hated the words "Happy Halloween."

Because as the kids from music class chased Bryce, they were joined by other kids, streaming out of their classrooms with chocolate on their lips, chanting, "Forbidden! Forbidden! Forbidden!"

Sweat dripped down Bryce's face, washing away the green paint. The only place he thought it was safe to go was the Dungeon. So that's where he went. Through the halls, down the stairs, squeezing between the doorframe into the—

Sparkling clean bathroom?

This was not the Dungeon Bryce was in a few minutes before.

There was no stink, no rust, no dark, no dust. No squeaks or creaks. No graffiti on the wall that said: *Flush The Toilet + U Will B Sucked into the Burrito Dimension!*

Huh. The Burrito Dimension?

Questions bounced around Bryce's brain as he examined the transformed room.

There's a dimension of burritos and people can go there?

Is that how dimensions work?

What about other worlds? Or other universes?

Would that explain what's happening?

What if the world hadn't changed when I ate the fish stick?

What if eating the fish stick sent me to an entirely different world? An entirely different universe?

If I eat another fish stick will I end up in the burrito dimension, and have to battle guacamole monsters, or swim across an ocean of refried beans, or wear flour tortillas for underpants instead of—

Bryce was interrupted mid-thought by kids crashing into the Dungeon after him, and he had no choice but to test his theory.

He held his nose, stuffed a fish stick in his mouth, chewed, and swallowed.

The world went blurry for a moment and then—

Chapter Eight

THE MULTIVERSE, INFINITY, AND FISH STICKS

Before we find out what happened to Bryce, let's talk about the multiverse for a moment. You know about the multiverse, right?

Don't worry if you don't. At least one version of you does.

"Version of me?" you might be thinking. "But I'm the only me. I'm unique. It's not like there are clones of me running around."

That's true, but we're not talking about clones. We're talking about multiple universes. We'll explain.

You live on Earth. Or one would assume you do. There's a small possibility that this book has been launched into outer space and it landed on a faraway planet and you're an alien of such great intelligence that you understand how to read Earth languages. In that case, you probably already know about multiple universes, so feel free to skip the rest of this chapter.

As for the rest of you—earthlings, in other words—you live on Earth. Earth revolves around the sun. The sun is the star at the center of our solar system. Our solar system contains planets like

Mars, Jupiter, and, depending on who you ask, Pluto. The hundreds of billions of stars (and their solar systems) that are closest to our sun make up our galaxy, the Milky Way. Beyond the Milky Way, there are hundreds of billions of galaxies—some bigger, some smaller—that make up our universe.

In other words, our universe is HUMONGOUS!

But what lies beyond our universe? Is there anything more?

Well, some people believe in the multiverse. It's a theory that proposes that our universe is just one universe out of multiple universes. Out of infinite universes, in fact!

Infinite universes are universes that go on . . . forever! Which basically means universes of every shape and size and configuration that you can think of. Plus never-ending other universes you can't even begin to fathom.

There could be a universe that's made entirely of chicken noodle soup. Because sure, why not?

Or one where a single wombat controls

everything and we all worship that wombat. Praise the almighty wombat and his magical cubical poop!

Or one where the only difference between it and our universe is that everyone in this other universe thinks that waterslides are boring. That's it. That's the only difference. Waterslides = booooring. Otherwise, identical.

That's the thing about infinity. EVERYTHING is possible.

Infinity is a hard concept to fit into your brain, isn't it?

Think of the biggest number you can. Add one to that. Bigger number, right?

Now double that number. Even bigger, huh?

Now multiply the new number by itself. Now multiply *that* new number by itself. Again. Again! AGAIN!

KEEP MULTIPLYING NEW NUMBERS BY THEMSELVES FOR THE REST OF YOUR LIFE!

Are you close to infinity now?

Nope. You are no closer to infinity now than when you started. Yikes. What a way to waste a life.

Here's the thing: you will never be close to infinity. Ever.

Infinity is the worst, isn't it?

Or maybe it's the best.

It depends on your point of view.

Because you see, Bryce's fish sticks were a bridge to infinite universes.

Take a bite, zip over to another reality. Locker 37 was wise enough not to send Bryce to any universes where he couldn't survive. After all, drowning in chicken noodle soup is no fate that any fourth-grader should endure. So there were infinite inhospitable universes that Bryce couldn't travel to. And yet there were also infinite universes that he could visit.

Yes, some infinities are bigger than other infinities and some infinities can fit inside other infinities and it's all very . . . confusing.

Don't worry about it, though.

Worry about this:

Chapter Nine

THE KIDOCRACY

The Dungeon changed back to the version Bryce was comfortable with: the uncomfortable version. Stinky, rusty, dark, dusty, etc.

The mob was gone. Bryce prayed that everything else was back to normal again, too.

He checked the mirror. His cracked reflection showed him that he was still wearing his green Skittle costume. But someone else was in the Dungeon with him.

"Oh, hi, Mr. Dodd," Mr. Rao, the art teacher, said as he stepped out of a stall. In his hand, he had a Sharpie. He looked exceedingly nervous, perhaps as nervous as Bryce was.

"Greetings, Mr. Rao," Bryce said.

If everything was back to normal, then Bryce knew that Mr. Rao would send him straight back to Vice Principal Meehan's office. But he didn't. Instead, Mr. Rao hid the Sharpie behind his back. And in a whimpering voice he asked, "Am I . . . am I . . . in a pickle?"

Bryce didn't quite understand what Mr. Rao meant by "in a pickle," so he responded by saying, "It depends."

"Depends on what?"

"On if you're a cucumber. You're not a cucumber, are you, Mr. Rao? Or an onion? Or an egg? A fish of some sort?"

Mr. Rao, who had been staring bewilderedly at Bryce as he listed off all the different things that could be pickled, finally said, "What I mean is, am I in trouble? I don't have a bathroom pass. And I'm in the Dungeon." Then he clasped his hands together around the Sharpie like he was praying. "Please please please don't send me to Vice Principal Barnes."

Vice Principal Barnes? The only person that Bryce knew with the last name Barnes was—

"You don't mean Hunter, do you?"
Bryce asked.

A terrified look fell over Mr. Rao's face,
then he dropped the Sharpie, shrieked,
and ran out of the Dungeon. Which was
odd, to say the least.

You know what was also odd? The
fresh graffiti Bryce found in the toilet
stall Mr. Rao was just using. It read:
ADULTS RULE, KIDS DROOL.

Did Mr. Rao write that? It didn't seem
like something he'd write, and yet there it
was, in fresh Sharpie ink.

It ultimately didn't matter. Bryce
wasn't in trouble. That was the most
important thing.

And when he stepped out of the
Dungeon, everything else appeared

normal. That was also true when he walked up the stairs and into the halls. Same doors, same posters, same janitor's closet that Bryce knew so well. But when he glanced into the classrooms, he could hardly believe his eyes.

Children were the teachers and adults were the students.

In the art room, the usually timid Carson was standing in front of Mr. Gregson and other teachers. The teachers were sitting on stools with canvases, paints, and mounds of clay in front of them. Carson was confidently telling them to create self-portraits. "No mirrors, no phones, use your mind's eye, people. Your mind's eye."

In the gym, the rule-breaker Riley had

a whistle around her neck, and she was calling the shots. "Holy rigatoni, everyone, it's time for CIRCUS TENT!" she yelled as Bryce's regular gym teacher, Mr. Trundle, and a bunch of other adults scrambled underneath a puffed-up, rainbow-colored parachute.

In Bryce's homeroom, the brilliant Keisha James was standing at the whiteboard, where a math formula was projected. $E=mc^2$ it read. "Time is relative," Keisha said.

Mrs. Shen, Bryce's homeroom teacher, was among the teachers sitting at the desks in the classroom. She raised her hand and asked, "Does that mean that time is my ... cousin?"

Keisha shook her head in sympathy.

"It's relative, as in the theory of relativity. You're not related to it."

"So, like . . . a stepsister?" Mrs. Shen asked.

Bryce didn't want to watch any more of this. This was the first time he had ever felt smarter than Mrs. Shen. He couldn't handle that feeling.

And he couldn't handle the sound of the next voice he heard.

"Hey, Bryce, nice costume. What are you, a booger?"

He turned around to see who it was. A boy wearing a suit stood in the hall.

"Whoa," Bryce said. "You're . . . you're . . . Hunter."

Hunter grinned a wicked grin and said, "The one and only. Meet me in my office. I want to talk to you."

Chapter Ten

VICE PRINCIPAL BARNES

Hunter Barnes led Bryce into Vice Principal Meehan's office. Actually, that's not correct. It was Hunter Barnes's office in this particular universe, and he was known as *Vice Principal Barnes*. No joke. It even said so on the door.

Everything inside looked like Vice

Principal Meehan's office, but Hunter sat behind the desk. And Bryce stood in front of it, just like he had earlier that morning.

"Why are you dressed so weird, Bryce?" Hunter asked. "Are you teaching your students about how to embarrass themselves?"

Bryce didn't see anything embarrassing about his costume. Maybe it was a bit weird, but it was also very nice. Weird, but nice—exactly like Bryce was. Not that he would say that to Hunter. Weird things and nice things were bullies' favorite targets.

So Bryce simply said, "I'm a Skittle."

"Look more like a booger," Hunter said. "But your teaching methods have always been . . . different."

"So, I'm a teacher, huh?" Bryce asked.

"Because in this universe, everything is wacky backward, right? Like, kids are teachers and teachers are students?"

"In this universe?" Hunter said. "How many other universes are there, ya weirdo?"

"From what I've experienced, it's somewhere between three and infinity," Bryce said.

Hunter sighed. "I should laser you for being such a weirdo. But I'm not allowed. And even if I was, I'd have to deal with Keisha James complaining to the school board about it."

"Really? She'd do that for me?" Bryce asked, because he always assumed Keisha only paid attention to him when she was embarrassed for him. Knowing that she would stick up for him literally warmed his heart.

Bryce wanted to know more, but Hunter didn't elaborate. Instead, he sniffed the air and asked, "Is that . . . fish sticks?"

"Ummm . . ."

Hunter sniffed some more. "It is. It is fish sticks. Hand 'em over, Bryce!"

"But Riley is the only person I know who likes fish sticks," Bryce said.

Hunter laughed. "Nice try, booger boy. I need those fish sticks."

Bryce looked down into his costume. The fish sticks were still on the plate and still steaming hot. "I'm not sure you want these ones. They're . . . powerful."

"Of course, fish sticks are powerful," Hunter said. "What else do you think charges up my laser nose?"

"Your laser nose?" Bryce said.

Hunter smiled and said, "You want to see it again, don't you?"

"Um, sure," Bryce said, but he clearly wasn't sure.

"I only have one charge left, so do you want me to laser a student or that plant over there?" Hunter asked as he pointed to a potted fern in the corner.

Laser a student? That didn't sound particularly nice. So Bryce said, "I'm gonna go with the plant."

"Oh, you're no fun, but coming right up," Hunter said, as he pointed the tip of his nose at the plant. Then he pinched both his earlobes and pulled them down.

A blue laser shot from Hunter's nose—

zaaaap!—and hit the fern dead center.
The fern burst into flame. And Hunter
burst into laughter.

"Go get a student," he said between
cackles. "I haven't lasered a student in
forever. But I think it's time. Maybe

that Greg Gregson guy. But I'll need to recharge by eating those fish sticks first."

Bryce didn't blink. What kind of universe was this? It was a universe where he didn't get in trouble for wearing his costume and where kids had all the power. But it was also one where Hunter was in charge. And where Hunter had a laser nose.

Which meant it was an awful universe.

So Bryce reached down into his costume and pulled out the fish sticks.

"Thanks, booger boy," Hunter said as he grabbed for them.

But Bryce was too fast. He took a bite. The world went blurry.

Chapter Eleven

THE FACE BEHIND THE TREE

Bryce was in a forest. The ground was covered in colorful leaves. The trees swayed in a gentle breeze. Birds chirped. It was chilly, but pleasant.

Hopewell Elementary was gone. There was no vice principal's office. No gym or cafetorium. There were no buildings anywhere. It was just forest as far as the eye could see.

He still had his fish sticks with him. They seemed to follow him to whatever universe he visited. And he was still wearing his costume. Those seemed to be the only things that stayed consistent no matter what universe he was in. Plus he wasn't in trouble for wearing his costume, so that was a good thing.

But he also wasn't sure if he should be in a universe where Hopewell Elementary didn't exist. Fourth grade was important. Without fourth grade, there'd be no fifth grade, and without fifth grade, there'd be no sixth grade, and without—

You get the point. But it was about more than academics for Bryce. It was about friends and fellow students. Where was Carson? And Riley? What about Keisha?

Where was anybody?

The answer to that last question came in the form of a familiar sounding voice behind him.

"Hello, Skittle," the voice said.

Bryce quickly turned around to discover a face poking out from behind a tree. But it wasn't a human face.

"You're a . . . ," Bryce said, but he couldn't finish his sentence. Because he was staring at a gummy bear. It was at least four feet tall, and it was blue and, for lack of a better word, gummy. It was also moving and talking.

"It's been years since I've chatted with a Skittle," the gummy bear said.

"Well, I've never ever *ever* chatted with a gummy bear," Bryce said, with a mix of fear and joy in his voice.

The gummy bear put out a soft and jiggly paw, and said, "Now you have. My name is Carson. Carson Cooper."

"It can't be," Bryce said as he reached out and shook the soft and jiggly paw.

"It can and it is," the gummy bear said in a voice that sounded exactly like the Carson that Bryce knew. "The others will be so excited to meet you."

"There are more like you?" Bryce asked.

"Sure, there are," Gummy Carson said. "Follow me."

Chapter Twelve

GUMMY BEAR PICNIC

Gummy Carson led Bryce around a thick patch of trees and past a field full of rocks. One of the rocks reminded him of a rock from the playground that kids always tripped over. In fact, it looked exactly like it.

They walked a little farther, following a path through pricker bushes until they came upon more gummy bears, who sat in a circle around a glowing hole in the ground. It almost looked like a firepit, but it was clearly a glowing hole.

All the gummy bears turned and smiled when they saw Bryce.

"Hey, everyone," Gummy Carson said. "I met a Skittle. His name is . . ."

"Bryce," Bryce said.

"Hi, Bryce, I'm Riley," said a red gummy bear.

"And I'm Keisha," said a green gummy bear.

It was incredible. They all looked like gummy bears, but they had the names and voices of kids he knew. What were the odds?

The odds were quite slim, but when there are infinite universes, odds don't mean much. A universe like this had to exist, and Bryce figured he might as well enjoy it. He had always wanted to talk to gummy bears.

"We were about to have a picnic,"

Gummy Carson told Bryce. "And we'd love it if you joined us."

"Oh, please do," Gummy Keisha added. "It's been so long since I've enjoyed the company of a Skittle. I adore Skittles."

Everyone was so friendly that Bryce immediately stopped thinking of them as gummy bears. He started thinking of them as friends. Even Keisha, who wasn't technically his friend in his home universe. And that felt simply wonderful.

Bryce sat down with his friends in the circle, which gave him a closer view of the hole. The glow from it was orange, but it didn't seem to give off any heat. "So, what's with the hole?" he asked.

"Oh, that's a very important hole," Gummy Carson said.

"A most magical hole," Gummy Riley said with a paw up. "It solves problems."

"I can solve most problems on my own," Gummy Keisha added. "But when I can't, this hole does the trick."

It sounded very familiar to Bryce, so he said, "We have something like that where I come from. It's called Locker 37."

"Ooooh, sounds very lockery," Gummy Riley said.

"Where do you come from?" Gummy Keisha asked. "Is it a place where only Skittles live?"

"There are Skittles there, sure," Bryce said. "Lots of other stuff, too."

"What do you eat there?" Gummy Carson asked. "I just realized that we were about to have a picnic, but we don't know what Skittles eat. I'm worried we won't have what you like. All we eat are onions. Onion soup. Onion rings. Onion tarts."

"That's *tarta de cebolla* en Español," Gummy Riley said.

Not only were these talking gummy bears, but they were also bilingual gummy bears. Very impressive!

"Onions are okey-dokey by me," Bryce said, trying to be polite. But he was not a fan of onion soup, onion rings, or onion tarts. Not that he'd ever had an onion tart. Still, he could confidently say he was not a fan.

Gummy Keisha put a gooey paw on Bryce's shoulder and said, "Don't worry, buddy. You don't have to eat onions if you don't want to. And I can tell you don't want to. Just think of your favorite food and the hole will give it to you. It's that simple."

It was an intriguing idea. Plus Bryce was quite hungry, having skipped breakfast that morning to prepare his costume.

So what food did Bryce think about?

Chapter Thirteen

DO NOT THINK ABOUT UNICORNS

Controlling your thoughts is a hard thing to do. Want proof?

For the next minute, DO NOT think about unicorns.

Seriously. Close your eyes for one minute and try NOT to think about unicorns. You know, with their flowing manes and the rainbow sparkles in their eyes? DO NOT think about any of that. At all. Think about anything in the universe besides unicorns.

Got it?

Good.

Go.

. . .

Couldn't do it, could you? Unicorns kept sneaking back into your thoughts, didn't they? You were probably sitting there thinking about the vastness of the universe, and imagining the endless void of space when all of a sudden, a unicorn in an astronaut's helmet floated by and waved its hoof at you. Don't worry. It happens to everyone.

It happened to Bryce. Gummy Keisha had asked him to think of his favorite food so that the magical hole would give him his favorite food. But Bryce didn't want to think of his favorite food.

It was not because his favorite food was unicorns. Because *ewww*, gross!

Or maybe not gross. Maybe unicorns are delicious. Maybe they taste like chocolate and peanut butter, or cheese puffs, or strawberry and kiwi smoothies. We'll never know, of course, because the last remaining unicorns left our planet in 1969 when they stowed away on the first rocket to the moon.

Wait. We've been distracted by unicorns again, haven't we? What were we talking about?

Oh yes. Bryce's favorite food.

It was something very different from unicorns. He wanted to hide the idea of his favorite food away in that drab sealed container at the back of his brain. In other words, he didn't want to think about it.

So, of course, he thought about it.

Chapter Fourteen

FAVORITE FOOD

A gummy bear popped out of the glowing orange hole.

Not a big talking gummy bear. A regular gummy bear that you'd find in any candy store. Because this was Bryce's favorite food, and he couldn't *not* think about his favorite food. But it certainly created an awkward situation.

Gummy Keisha gasped, put a paw on

her chest and said, "That's not . . . ?"

"It's a baby!" Gummy Carson screamed. "The Skittle wants to eat a baby!"

Bryce scrambled to his feet and put his hands up. "I do not want to eat any babies. That's candy. It's not alive."

"It's . . . dead?" Gummy Carson said with a gulp. And then he fainted.

"Holy Pasta Frutta," Gummy Riley whispered. "Things have gotten pretty dark pretty quickly, haven't they?"

"Where I come from, these are candy," Bryce said frantically as he picked the little gummy bear up. "Taste it and you'll see. It's like if I ate a Sour Patch Kid. I eat Sour Patch Kids all the time."

"Um . . . what does that Skittle eat all the time?" said a voice coming from the forest. Then a walking, talking Sour Patch Kid stepped into the light.

Bryce set the gummy bear down. "I should probably leave, shouldn't I?"

All the big gummy bears nodded. Gummy Keisha's face twisted up in anger, and she pointed to the dark forest. And the Sour Patch Kid took a step back as

Bryce skulked past him.

The last thing he heard from the crowd as he walked away was absolutely devastating. He heard the voice of Gummy Keisha, which was the exact same voice as the Keisha he knew from home. She was saying, "That was a close call. I'm so glad I never have to see that weirdo again. And I used to like Skittles, too. Never again."

Chapter Fifteen
CHECKLIST

Bryce walked slowly through the forest, considering his dilemma. He knew he could eat some fish sticks and travel to a different universe, but that's not what he needed right now. He needed to think, and the forest was a pleasant place to do that.

Bryce was beginning to notice a pattern. The fish sticks were supposed to solve his problem. He thought his problem was that he wanted to wear his costume and not get in trouble for it. In each universe he had visited, that problem had been solved. No one was mad about his costume. But in each universe he had visited, new problems replaced that old one. He had faced bloodthirsty mobs, laser noses, and disgusted gummy bears.

He had a sudden realization. Maybe Locker 37 was giving him access to all the different universes where his problem was solved so that he could choose which one he liked best. Therefore, when he found the ideal fit, he could stop eating the fish sticks and settle down there. After all, wouldn't everyone want to live in a universe where they didn't have to think about some of the things they didn't want to think about? It seemed better than going home.

The idea was scary, but also incredibly exciting. What would Bryce's ideal universe look like? He knew he couldn't expect perfection, but he thought it might be helpful to have a list of things his ideal world would include, so when he found one that fit the bill, he'd be happy enough to stay.

The plate of fish sticks came with a mound of ketchup, so Bryce dipped a finger in it and wrote his list on the cardboard inside of his costume.

1. **Costumes:** That was his original problem, right? In his ideal universe, costumes, of all shapes and sizes, needed to be acceptable. Celebrated, in fact. And people had to be okay with using the word Halloween.

2. **Family:** He loved his mom and dad and his grandparents and all his aunts and uncles and cousins and he couldn't imagine a universe without them.

3. **Friends:** The same went for his friends. Riley and Carson had to be there. What about Keisha? Yes, Bryce couldn't exactly call her a friend. But

he knew he wanted her there. He'd even be okay with Hunter being there, as long as he didn't have a laser nose.

4. **Hopewell Elementary:** Sometimes he didn't like going to school, but that didn't mean he didn't love his school. Or need his school. Love is confusing like that. No matter what, Hopewell Elementary had to stay, too.

5. **Gummy Bears That Don't Walk and Talk:** That's pretty much self-explanatory.

When it came down to it, Bryce wasn't asking for much. Or was he?

Chapter Sixteen

THE BALLAD OF THE SCREAMIN' BEAGLES

Before we answer that question, it's time for a quick detour. It's time to tell the story of Gregory Gregson. Don't worry, it won't take long.

Gregory Gregson was a weird, but nice, kid. Having almost the exact same first and last name wasn't what made him weird, but that didn't *not* make him weird. The kids in his class all called him Greg Greg. He was okay with that, even though some did it to tease him.

Greg Greg went to Hopewell Elementary about thirty years before Bryce did. When he began fourth grade, he learned about Locker 37, like every other fourth-grader at school. And when he entered fifth grade, he forgot about it, like every other fifth-grader did.

It was a shame, perhaps. Because it meant he didn't remember the morning when he opened Locker 37 up and found a tambourine inside. Which was maybe the most important moment of his life.

The fateful day started with a problem. No snow! The day before, the weather forecast had predicted snow, but no snow had fallen anywhere close to

Hopewell Elementary by the morning. No snow meant no snow day, which meant fourth graders had to go to school. There weren't a lot of smiles in the hallways.

"I'll fix it," Greg Greg announced, and he hurried to Locker 37.

When he opened the locker, he found a tambourine inside the orange glow. He shook it and slapped it and patted it against his thigh, making the little cymbals jingle. Then he looked out the nearest window.

Still no snow.

"Oh well," Greg Greg said. "I guess magic can't solve everything."

But the other fourth-graders were furious. They surrounded him in the hall before classes started.

"You said you'd make it snow!" Lucinda Honeycutt shouted.

"Yeah, what gives?" Beatrice Vonderhauf asked. "Why are we still at school? You wasted Locker 37, didn't you, Greg Greg?"

Greg Greg shrugged and said, "The tambourine makes a nice sound, at least." Then he patted it against his hip.

As soon as he did, the other kids started dancing. They couldn't control it. Their heads started bobbing, their toes started tapping, and their hands swayed from side-to-side. But once he stopped playing the tambourine, they stopped dancing.

"What just happened?" Lucinda asked.

"I think we might've had . . . fun?"
Beatrice said.

Beatrice was right. Dancing was fun.
And for the rest of the day, whenever
Greg Greg saw another fourth-grader
who was sad, or angry, or not enjoying
school, he played the tambourine. And a
dance party broke out.

Some teachers were a little annoyed, but it didn't distract students from the school work. In fact, kids were so happy to be at school that they worked harder and paid closer attention. No one was dozing off in class, that's for sure. And no one cared anymore about the lack of a snow day. It was the greatest moment of Greg Greg's life up to that point.

That night, when Greg Greg went home, he knew that he couldn't count on having a magical tambourine again. But he realized that he could learn to play other instruments. He didn't need magic to start more dance parties. He simply needed some passion. He had plenty of that.

The next day, he posted a handmade sign in the halls. It read:

WANT TO JOIN A BAND BUT DON'T KNOW HOW TO PLAY AN INSTRUMENT? THAT'S OKAY. LET'S LEARN TOGETHER! JOIN THE SCREAMIN' EAGLES TODAY!

Greg Greg called the band the Screamin' Eagles as a tribute to his father and grandfather, who were also named Gregory Gregson. They were both part of 101st Airborne Division of the army, which was referred to as, you guessed it, the Screaming Eagles.

But the name of Greg Greg's band didn't last long. It was changed a few minutes after he posted the sign, when a graffiti artist named Sammy Rao took a

Sharpie to it and added a B to the name. Therefore the Screamin' Eagles became the Screamin' Beagles. And Greg Greg was okay with that. In fact, he thought the new name sounded even better.

Two people joined the Screamin' Beagles that week.

The first was a boy named Darius Schnell, who was encouraged to join by his father, Phineas Schnell, a professional physicist and an amateur theremin enthusiast. (If you don't know what a theremin is, look it up. It's pretty cool.)

The second was Beatrice Vonderhauf, who had such a good time dancing to the tambourine that she decided she wanted more music in her life.

The trio stuck together for the next thirty years, teaching and encouraging one another to play with passion and joy. None of them remembered that it all started because of a magical locker, an enchanted tambourine, and a snow day that never came to be.

All they knew was somewhere along the way, they fell in love with music and it was as important to them as anything.

Chapter Seventeen

WEIRD NEW PLACE

Now, what does any of that have to do with Bryce?

Well, the Screamin' Beagles were Bryce's favorite band, of course.

And Greg Greg was Bryce's music teacher. Though Bryce knew him as Mr. Gregson.

But perhaps the most important thing to note is that when Bryce took a bite of his fish sticks in the gummy bear universe, he was transported to another universe, one where he was onstage in the Hopewell Elementary cafetorium, and he was a part of the Screamin' Beagles.

Seriously.

He was standing in front of hundreds of kids who were all wearing Halloween costumes, and who were cheering and clapping along to music . . . that Bryce was playing!

He was holding a bass guitar, and even though he didn't know how to play a bass guitar, he was picking at the strings and— *dum, da dum dum*—music was coming out. Music that sounded good!

Bryce looked down and saw that he was still wearing his green Skittle costume.

Then he looked over his shoulder at his bandmates. They weren't Beatrice Vonderhauf or Darius Schnell. Mr. Gregson was nowhere to be seen. Riley and Carson were there instead. Riley was dressed as a Ping-Pong ball and was playing drums. Carson was dressed as a giant pink eraser and was playing guitar.

Even though this was an entirely new lineup for the band, Bryce was sure they were the Screamin' Beagles. The band's logo of a howling beagle was painted on the drum set, as well as on the banner that hung above them, which said, "Happy Halloween from the Screamin' Beagles!"

Plus, they were playing one of the Screamin' Beagles' best original songs, "Weird New Place." They were on the

second verse, and Riley was singing.

I'm lost without you by my side,
All I want is to run and hide.
You disappeared without a trace,
Take me with you to a weird new place.

It felt amazing, especially when the crowd all held up little flashlights and started to sing along with the chorus. It was so loud that it rattled the vents in the ceiling.

Weird new place!
Weirder than outer space!
Weird new place!
Makin' my bloodstream race!
Weird new place!
Puts me in a state of grace!
Ain't nowhere else I'd rather be than a . . .
Weird! New! Place!

Before the song was even over, the costumed crowd rushed the stage, but it wasn't scary like the mob that chased Bryce earlier that day. They adored him and Riley and Carson. They picked them up and carried them around the cafetorium as they chanted, "Beagles! Beagles! Beagles!"

When they brought Bryce toward the exit, he noticed his parents were standing near the kitchen, and they were smiling and waving. It made him feel even better. They were proud of their son. And it made his checklist complete.

Costumes? Check.

Family? Check.

Friends? Check.

Hopewell Elementary? Check.

No angry classmates . . . no laser noses . . . no talking gummy bears? Check.

Bryce smiled widely as they led him into the hall. He could see living here.

Chapter Eighteen

NUMBER ONE FAN

The new lineup of the Screamin' Beagles sat in comfortable chairs in the teachers' lounge. They were drinking lemonade and watching a video of their performance on a giant TV.

"This is the life, huh?" Bryce said to Riley and Carson.

"Holy strozzapreti, you can say that again," Riley replied.

And Carson simply smiled and took a long sip of his lemonade through a straw.

There was a knock on the door.

"Enter!" Riley called out.

The door opened, and there was Keisha. She didn't seem to be in a costume. She was wearing jeans and a T-shirt with the letters *S* and *B* on it.

"What are you dressed as?" Bryce asked.

"What I'm always dressed as," Keisha said. "The Screamin' Beagles number one fan! You write the best songs ever!"

In his original universe, Bryce was the Screamin' Beagles' number one fan. And he figured it was only polite to pay homage to the actual founders of the band.

"You should really be celebrating the true genius behind it all," Bryce said. "Mr. Gregson."

"Who?" the three others said at the same time.

"The music teacher, Gregory Gregson," Bryce said. "He started the Screamin' Beagles with Darius Schnell and Beatrice Vonderhauf."

"I have literally never heard of any of those names," Keisha said.

"Me, neither," Carson said.

"Yeah, those sound like a bunch of nobodies," Keisha said. "I prefer celebrating the three of you. What can I do for you to make your day brighter?"

Keisha smiled, which was usually enough to make Bryce's day brighter, but it didn't this time.

"Shouldn't you be focused on school?" Bryce said. "What about extracurricular activities? Aren't you the president of the Junior Janitor Club?"

Keisha waved him off and said, "I prefer skipping school. And clubs are for fools. Hey, that rhymes. Maybe you can put it in one of your songs. *Skip school. Clubs are for fools.*"

It hurt Bryce to hear Keisha talk like this. This was not the same honest and dedicated girl he admired so much.

It also hurt Bryce to know that the people who created the Screamin' Beagles, the ones who had worked so hard for so many years, didn't exist in this universe. Or if they did, they certainly weren't getting credit for the songs they wrote.

That was because they didn't write those songs in this universe. Bryce, Riley, and Carson did. With infinite universes, this reality was an inevitability. But it didn't mean Bryce had to like it.

His checklist needed revision. Bryce dipped his finger into the ketchup on the fish stick plate. He wasn't sure what exactly to write as number six on his checklist. And as he thought about it, he didn't notice a hand reaching inside his costume and grabbing a fish stick.

"Oh, yummy," Riley said.

And she took a bite of one of the fish sticks.

Chapter Nineteen

IMPORTANT BEAGLE BUSINESS

Riley's eyes went blank for a moment. Then her face went through a series of contortions. Finally, she shook her head like she was getting water out of her ear, and took a deep breath.

"Well, how about that?" she said as she gazed down at her hand. The fish stick she had bitten was now gone.

"What just happened to you?" Carson asked.

Riley ignored him. Instead, she examined the room until she spotted Bryce. Then she grabbed him by the wrist and said, "So you *were* telling the truth. Come with me."

She led him out of the teachers' lounge and down the hall, where the kids and teachers all cheered and begged for autographs.

"Can't stop now," Riley told them. "Important Beagle business to attend to."

They were devoted, but respectful, fans. They all took a step back and cleared the way so that Riley could bring Bryce around the corner and all the way to . . .

"Locker 37," Bryce said, staring at the locker that got him here in the first place.

"Open it," Riley said.

"I . . . I . . . I . . ."

"Don't worry, the combination is the same in this universe as it is in your universe."

"You know about the multiple universes?"

Riley smiled. "Open the locker."

Bryce followed her command, using the combination that every fourth-grader from Hopewell Elementary in his universe had memorized. And sure enough, the locker opened. Inside, he found . . .

"Nothing," he said.

"Exactly," Riley said. "In this universe, Locker 37 is not magical at all. But your fish sticks sure are. Do you know how many universes I visited after I took that bite?"

Bryce guessed the same number that he had visited. "Four?"

Riley shook her head and said, "Try fifty million, seven hundred sixty-five thousand, five hundred and forty. Give or take."

"That's . . . more than four."

Riley sat down with her legs crossed and said, "Have a seat, Bryce. I'm about to blow your mind."

Chapter Twenty

MIND, BLOWN

Reader: Please keep something in mind. This chapter is told in Riley's voice, so imagine that Riley is saying all this stuff, and not the esteemed author, who uses much more refined and proper language and grammar. You have been warned.

Listen up, Bryce. Here's how it went down.

Those fish sticks of yours are the real deal. Seriously. I took a bite and poof, I was in another universe.

I didn't know it was another universe at first. At first I thought I had food poisoning and I was imagining the army of ten-foot-tall Madagascar hissing cockroaches chasing me through the halls of school. But when they started to gnaw on my foot, you better believe I wised up.

I took another bite, and things changed again. Next, I was in a universe where everyone looked exactly like me. Rileys everywhere.

Paradise, right? Nope. It got boring after a few minutes because we all kept on trying to prank each other, but no one was falling for the pranks. Bummer. I took a bite of the fish stick and left that universe, too.

I ended up in a place where dogs were cats and cats were hamsters and hamsters were giraffes and they all spoke French and it was very confusing, Bryce, very confusing. So another bite and I left that universe as well.

That's when I realized that I needed to make my fish stick last. I'd eaten half of it already. If I ate the whole thing, I might get stuck in a world I didn't like. And that's how I began my awesome quest to find the perfect world. One where there was only one Riley, but fish sticks and pranking were plentiful.

Instead of biting the fish stick, I just touched it to my tongue whenever I wanted to jump to another universe. And I hopped from universe to universe, getting into adventures, meeting wacky and wonderful creatures, educating and terrifying myself with the mysteries of time and space. As well as discovering the secret to immortality. You know how it is.

As you might've guessed, you can only lick a fish stick for so long before it dissolves. So, soon I figured out how to suck single molecules off it, one at a time, using a technique that a talking thermos taught me. That kept my adventures going. I traveled to other planets. I got sucked into black holes. I even ran into you again, Bryce, and we had some spooky and delicious fun. Don't worry, you'll get to that part soon enough.

But I never found perfection. Finally, all the molecules ran out and the fish stick was gone, and I ended up, well, here. Today. Back where I started.

Pretty cool, huh?

Chapter Twenty-One
MUST FEEL RIGHT

"That's quite a story," Bryce said. "You really got sucked into black holes?"

Riley shrugged. "Plenty of times."

"Does it . . . tickle?"

"Not really. Waterslides are more fun."

"So, how old are you exactly?" Bryce asked.

Riley used her finger to write invisible

math equations in the air, and she whispered to herself before saying to Bryce, "Either I'm 195,292 years old . . . or I'm ten. Depending on your point of view."

"You mean like if I climb a hill or something?"

Riley let out a little snort and said, "No, I mean I'm back to my original universe and picking up where I left off when I was ten, so . . ."

"But how do you know this is your original universe?"

Riley smiled at Bryce. "Trust me. It just feels right."

Bryce looked down at his fish sticks. Riley had traveled to over fifty million universes on one fish stick alone. He had at least ten fish sticks left. That meant he could visit half a billion universes!

"So are you thinking it's time to move on?" Riley asked.

Bryce considered this. It was nice to be part of the Screamin' Beagles, but it wasn't the life he wanted. It simply didn't feel right. He dipped his finger in the ketchup and wrote number six on his list.

6. Must Feel Right

It was hard to say what "right" was at the moment. But this place wasn't it.

"It was a pleasure meeting this version of you, Riley," Bryce said, and he stuck his ketchupy hand out to shake.

"Oh, don't worry. You'll be seeing me again," Riley said, and then she kicked him in the shins.

"Ow!" Bryce yelped as he grabbed

his shin and hopped on one foot. "That seemed unnecessary."

"No one shakes hands in this universe," Riley said with a shrug. "Shin-kicking is the traditional way to say goodbye."

As soon as Bryce recovered, he didn't kick Riley in the shins. Traditional or not, it didn't seem nice. But he did take a teensy tiny bite (a lick, really) of a fish stick.

Chapter Twenty-Two
LOCKER 37,000

The world went fuzzy, and when it became clear again, Bryce was standing alone in the hall next to Locker 37,000.

That's not a misprint. Locker 37,000 looked just like the Locker 37 from Bryce's universe, except for the three zeroes on its number plate.

The locker was open and empty. Bryce closed it quietly and decided to go exploring. But when he turned around, he spotted Carson walking toward him.

Carson was dressed as a fraction. Yes, a fraction, like you'd see in math class. His costume was a white sweat suit with a black seven on his shirt, two black ones on his pants, and a black belt in the middle.

He was 7/11 (or seven elevenths), in other words. But there was a slight problem with the fraction. It had cranberry juice on it.

"Can you believe it?" Carson said with a smile as he approached Locker 37,000. "Another stain. If Locker 37,000 can't help me, I hope you might have some pants you can lend me. Actually, who am I kidding? Locker 37,000 always helps!"

Carson was smiling wider than Bryce

had ever seen him smile. Not that Carson was normally sad, but he was nervous more often than not. So the smile was ... a good sign?

"Please don't tell me I'm in a universe where there are, like, little lizards inside your cheeks pushing them up and making it look like you're smiling," Bryce said. "You're actually happy, right Carson?"

"Who wouldn't be happy when there's Locker 37,000 here to solve all our problems?" Carson said, smiling wide enough that Bryce could confirm that there were indeed no lizards in his cheeks. Then Carson quickly turned the locker's combination dial, as if he'd done it countless times, gave the door a friendly tap with his elbow and opened it up.

There was an orange glow inside. Within that glow there was a small pink rubber eraser.

"Perfect," Carson said, as he grabbed it and immediately started rubbing his pants. The stain disappeared instantly, and so did the eraser.

"That was surprisingly uncomplicated," Bryce remarked.

And that's when another voice chimed in. "My turn!"

It was Keisha and she was standing at the end of the hall dressed as a butterfly. When Bryce saw her, he froze for a moment. Maybe it was her silky and colorful wings and the way she flapped them as she walked toward Locker 37,000, but she seemed so . . . stunning.

"Hey, buddy," she said to him as she placed a soft hand on his shoulder and then reached over to the combination dial. She spun the dial faster than Carson did, and when she opened the locker, it was glowing orange again. Instead of an eraser inside, there was a small clock.

This was interesting to Bryce, because in his universe, Locker 37 only gave out one object a day. It seemed Locker 37,000 was more generous.

"Are you solving a Junior Janitor Club problem?" Carson asked Keisha, referring to Keisha's favorite extracurricular activity in Bryce's original universe.

Keisha shook her head as she grabbed the clock and said, "Junior Janitor Club runs a tight ship. We don't have any problems. No, my problem is that I forgot to do my homework, if you can believe it."

"I can't," Carson said. "But I'm sure that clock will help."

"Time is now on my side," Keisha said, and she skipped away down the hall, her wings fluttering as she went. Bryce couldn't take his eyes off her. That is, until he had no choice but to look at what came down the hall next.

Riley came next. And she was dressed as a drone, if you can believe it. (And you can believe it, because that's what we're telling you: Riley was dressed as a drone.) But it wasn't some simple cardboard costume. It was a mechanical costume with metal and motors and actual working propellers.

That's right. Riley was literally flying

down the hall. And classical music was playing.

Dun, dunnn, dunnnnn . . . dun, dun, went the music.

And, "Holy vermicelli!" went Riley. "I didn't know Locker 37,000 would be so popular today. Ignore that I was even here, because there's going to be a . . . surprise later."

Then she turned the dial, opened the locker, shielded her eyes from the orange glow, and pulled out a ridiculous and wonderful rainbow hat.

"That's certainly unique," Bryce commented.

"But also predictable," Carson said.

Riley tucked the hat under her arm, and as she flew away, she shook her fist in the air, but in a playful way. "Don't call me predictable, Carson!" she shouted.

And Carson turned to Bryce and said, "I bet that hat will make clones of her and then she'll use those clones to pull off a prank. Typical Riley."

Then Carson chuckled, turned away, and headed off to class.

Chapter Twenty-Three

REALLY-GOOD-VERSE

School in the universe of Locker 37,000 was really good. This school was, at least. This version of Hopewell Elementary was full of happy kids in creative costumes, and they were all enthusiastic about learning. The lessons and the teachers were the same as in Bryce's home universe, but they felt more fun and important.

In math class, Mrs. Shen was cracking some of her better jokes, such as: "There are three kinds of people in the world: Those who can count and those who can't."

That's not to say everything was absolutely perfect. Hunter Barnes was still a bit of a bully. When he saw Bryce's green Skittle costume in math class, he said, "What are you? A green pea?" But that was still better than "booger boy."

In Bryce's locker, he found pictures of his family taped inside the door.

There were no giant talking gummy bears anywhere to be seen. There were no weird creatures of any type.

It felt like home here. In fact, it felt better than home.

But did it feel . . . right?

Bryce didn't know yet, but he thought he might stick around to see.

He wasn't sure how much time that might take. Or how much time he had. Or what time really meant when traveling to different universes.

Time is tricky like that. And you know what? Maybe it's a good time to talk about time.

Chapter Twenty-Four

DRIVING A HOT-DOG CAR THROUGH THE FOURTH DIMENSION

There's a really good book about time. You might have heard of it. It's called *Locker 37: The Rewindable Clock*. We don't want to spoil it so, if you haven't already, go read it right now. Don't worry, there's time.

In *Locker 37: The Rewindable Clock*, Mrs. Shen says that "time is change." Which is true. We mark time by how things in the universe change.

But time is something else, too. Time is also the fourth dimension.

What does that mean? Well, to understand it completely, we have to look at the first three dimensions. (Don't worry, none of them include the burrito dimension.)

Start by picturing a dot, like the period at the end of this sentence.

Or, better yet, take out a crayon, put its tip on a piece of paper, and draw a dot. Really. Do it.

Got that dot? Good. Don't lift that crayon yet. Because, hate to be the bearer of bad news, but your dot is dimensionless. What you need to do next is move the crayon across the page. Now you have a line. A line exists in . . .

The First Dimension! Have you ever heard someone refer to a character in a book as one-dimensional? That means there's not much to them. They're boring. Like a line, they have just one thing going for them. In the case of a character, that one thing might be that they juggle. That's it. Juggling is their only characteristic. In the case of a line, their only characteristic is length. Sorry line, but that isn't enough for us. We're moving on to . . .

The Second Dimension! To get there, you need to take your crayon and remove the wrapper. Now, place the crayon on top of the line you just drew. Press down and sweep or spin the crayon across the page in any direction.

Congratulations! You've drawn a shape! Maybe it's a square. Or perhaps you spun the crayon and created a circle. Heck, you might have moved it all around and made a squiggly thing that looks like a long and winding road. It doesn't matter. These are all two-dimensional shapes. In other words, they all have length AND width.

Two-dimensional things are flat like

one-dimensional things, but that doesn't mean they're boring. TVs, phones, tablets, and computers all entertain, educate, and inspire you using only two dimensions. In fact, some two-dimensional things are entertaining, educating, and inspiring you right now. The words in this book! They're totally two-dimensional!

(Unless, of course, you're listening to an audiobook version. In which case, we'd like the narrator to say the following word: floccinaucinihilipilification. Why? Just because.)

So yes, the second dimension has some versatility, but not as much as . . .

The Third Dimension! Otherwise

known as 3D! Don't worry, you don't need to put on any special glasses. All you have to do is imagine that the shape you drew is now sweeping downward and leaving behind a trail of shapes in the air below it. Like stacks of crayons underneath it melted together. Or like a 3D printer, and it's printing a solid object for you. It has length, width, and now, HEIGHT! So instead of a square, you have a cube. Instead of a circle, you have a cylinder or sphere. Instead of a flat squiggly thing, you have a . . . tall squiggly thing!

The third dimension is the dimension we all live in and are comfortable with. It's the dimension of beds and baseballs, sandwiches and skyscrapers, pygmy hippos and hippy pigs. We don't need to explain your everyday reality to you, so what we will try to do is explain . . .

The Fourth Dimension! Time. Time is the fourth dimension. Confusing, huh? Because time doesn't have a shape, like a line or a square or a grilled cheese sandwich, right? It doesn't fit in this sequence.

Or does it?

Now, this may be a little hard to wrap your brain around, but try to imagine that you could see in four dimensions. In other words, time isn't just something on an alarm clock reminding you to get out of bed. It's another direction you can see in.

Now picture a giant hot-dog-shaped car. (Your family has one of those in the driveway, right?) If you could see in four dimensions, you could see the hot-dog car's length, width, height, AND everything it's ever done and everywhere it's ever been! You can glance at it and see when it was being built in the factory, when it was driven to a hot-dog-eating contest, and when it was chased by the police, and the driver jumped out at the last second before it plunged to a fiery

doom in the Grand Canyon.

To put it another way, if the first dimension (a line) is created by the trail a dot leaves, and the second dimension (a shape) is created by the trail a line leaves, and the third dimension (an object) is created by the trail a shape leaves, then the fourth dimension (time) is created by the trail an object leaves. In other words, all the places the hot-dog-shaped car has ever been or will be.

But what comes after that? Is there . . .

The Fifth, Sixth, or Seventh Dimension? Many scientists believe there are actually ten dimensions, all wrapped around each other like some weird piece of cosmological pasta. Holy cosmolotoni! These ten dimensions explain the laws of pretty much everything. Big and small. Old and new. Everything that has been or ever could be.

If you master the ten dimensions, you can travel through space and time and between universes. Locker 37 was a master of all ten dimensions, and that's why these fish sticks were known as interdimensional fish sticks. (The author also wanted to write a book with the words interdimensional fish sticks in the title, so that's a factor, too.)

We won't get into all the details of interdimensionality at the moment, because we don't want to embarrass theoretical physicists by making it super easy for everyone to understand. Then they'd be out of a job.

For now, let's focus on those first four dimensions. All you need to know is that Bryce was a three-dimensional object, and he was leaving a four-dimensional trail through multiple universes.

But where did that trail lead? And could he turn around and travel back along it?

Chapter Twenty-Five

BRYCE'S TRAIL

Bryce decided to stay in the Locker 37,000 universe. He wasn't sure if it felt right yet. But it sure didn't feel wrong. He spent the rest of the day at school, where he enjoyed his classes and spending time with his friends. Then, he returned to his house for the evening, where he had a wonderful time seeing his family and trick-or-treating in his neighborhood.

Everything about this universe was like Bryce's universe, but better. The candy was more delicious. People like Keisha, who were sometimes annoyed and embarrassed by Bryce in his universe, were always friendly and supportive here. He slept more soundly.

That's right. He went to sleep in this universe. More than once! He was that comfortable. In fact, he stayed for more than three weeks. All the way until the end of November.

He no longer wore the Skittle costume, of course. Though, even if he had worn it, people wouldn't have cared. Everyone was so accepting.

On the last day of school before the Thanksgiving break, Hopewell

Elementary was serving a special lunch in the cafetorium. Turkey, mashed potatoes, and all the traditional Thanksgiving foods. Bryce had loaded up a full tray.

He also still had his plate of fish sticks—and they were somehow still steaming hot—but he kept them hidden in a lunch box. And he made sure he had his lunch box with him at all times.

It was sitting on the table next to him while he was eating his mashed potatoes and talking to Carson. He usually held onto the lunch box, but he was too busy using both his hands to describe how much stuffing he was planning to eat this year.

"About a googolplex times as much as this," he said with his arms stretched wide.

"Looks like you already have lunch,

so you won't be needing that," Hunter said as he walked by the table, picking up Bryce's lunch box. Bryce was quick to respond, but not quick enough.

He grabbed the lid of the lunch box, while Hunter grasped the handle. Pulling in opposite directions caused the box to open and the fish sticks to fly out.

"Staaaand baaack!" Bryce shouted. And as he did, one of the fish sticks somersaulted through the air . . .

It flipped once.

It flipped twice.

And then it hit him on the tongue.

His wonderful world went blurry.

Chapter Twenty-Six

NO!

"No!" Bryce shouted as the fish sticks fell to the ground and he found himself in another universe.

"No, no, no!" he shouted. For this was definitely not a wonderful universe.

It may have looked like a wonderful one at first glance. Because Bryce was now in a grand ballroom with chandeliers and dining tables. And that was nice.

But instead of people, the ballroom was full of tornadoes. And that was not nice!

No joke. This was a universe with small, self-contained tornadoes. And they were all dressed in evening gowns. And tuxedos! Imagine, if you can, fancy clothing with spinning vortexes coming out of the collars, sleeves, and pant legs. And if you can't imagine that, then take our word for it. It's strange and terrifying.

"No!" Bryce screamed again, and the tornadoes moved closer to him. Their vortexes spun a little faster. And the fish sticks started to slide across the floor toward the tornadoes, as if being sucked into a vacuum.

Bryce dove to grab the fish sticks, and could feel himself being pulled by the tornadoes. The tornadoes formed a circle. Soon they surrounded him on all sides, pulling his arms and legs and head in different directions.

The fish sticks were spinning on the floor, like helicopter blades. They were right in front of Bryce's face, but he couldn't move his arms, so he couldn't grab them. All he could do was fight fire with fire. Or fight suction with suction, that is.

Bryce pursed his lips and began to suck in air. The closest fish stick slowly stopped spinning and inched closer to him. This seemed to anger the tornadoes and so they spun faster. Bryce didn't have much room left in his lungs and he knew he couldn't do this for much longer. So, he decided to go for one last gasp. Or one last suck, that is.

All at once, he drew in as much breath as his lungs could hold, which was more than enough. An entire fish stick flew into his mouth and down his throat.

The tornado world went blurry.

He ended up in a new universe, but now he had one fewer fish stick. This universe was populated entirely by monkeys. Monkeys monkeys monkeys, as far as the eye could see.

Not chimpanzees, bonobos, orangutans, or gorillas. Those are apes. We're talking howler monkeys, capuchins, macaques, baboons, etc. They were wild and frantic and they shrieked and jumped and clung onto Bryce and stuffed two whole fish sticks down his throat.

Blurry.

And it kept happening.

Bryce kept trying to find his way back to the wonderful universe of Locker 37,000, but then he would end up traveling to some odd and dangerous universe. And instead of holding onto and conserving his fish sticks, he would end up eating them whole!

For instance . . .

He ate one while having a particularly vivid dream about ice cream in a universe where everyone slept for twenty-three hours a day.

He was tricked into swallowing three in one gulp by a rascally cartoon rabbit in a universe where cartoons and people lived together.

And he gobbled down two when

he ended up in a universe where the only things people ate were blue jeans. What else could he do? Denim was not delicious. And he was starving.

It eventually left him with one final fish stick. And it left him in a new universe.

Chapter Twenty-Seven

EMPTY

He was back in the Hopewell Elementary cafetorium, one he mostly recognized. But it was now entirely deserted.

Tables were flipped over. There were no people and not even a scrap of food anywhere. No tornadoes, monkeys, cartoons, or blue jeans either. A window at the back was broken, letting in a breeze that made the nutrition posters on the walls ripple.

Bryce didn't trust this cold and desolate universe. Raising his final fish stick to his mouth, he thought it might be best to lick it and test his luck yet again. Oh, what he would've given to be back in the universe with Locker 37,000. But he had no idea how to get back there, and he also couldn't risk ending up in a universe that was worse. He'd seen plenty of bad and strange ones already.

So he decided he should at least explore this universe for a bit, to be certain it wasn't a place he wanted to be. But he held tight to that fish stick, ready to lick it at a moment's notice.

The halls were as empty as the cafetorium, except for homework papers that lay scattered on the floor like autumn leaves. One stuck to his foot when he stepped on it, a science worksheet with Keisha's name on it.

Keisha! Seeing her name made him both happy and scared. Was she here, too? It didn't seem like anyone was here. At least not anymore. Something had obviously happened to anyone who was.

Something bad? Probably.

Well, when something bad happened, Bryce knew where to turn. He began to run, and in less than a minute he found himself standing in front of Locker 37. Not Locker 37,000. Just good old Locker 37.

As he dialed the combination, he said to himself, "I hope this works."

It did work.

The door opened.

But instead of an orange glow, something soft and rainbow colored was inside. It was a creature that had skin that rippled like fabric. It had swirling, glowing, rainbow eyes. It was beautiful and it was terrifying.

Before Bryce could even scream, the rainbow-colored creature jumped out of the locker. Bryce leapt backward and fell to the floor, dropping his fish stick. Then the creature grabbed his fish stick and escaped with it down the hall.

Chapter Twenty-Eight
THE RAINBOW SPECTER

Bryce recognized this creature. He was pretty sure he'd seen it before, and you can read all about the harrowing encounter in the blockbuster book, *Locker 37: The Ridiculous and Wonderful Rainbow Hat*. But feel free to finish this book first.

The creature was known as the Rainbow Specter. It was like a ghost who wore a sheet with all the colors of the rainbow on it. It was supposedly quite dangerous. Bryce had heard that if he touched it, he might end up like a marshmallow that had been zapped in a microwave.

He needed his fish stick back, which meant he had no choice but to face the danger and chase it. So Bryce started running as fast as he could down the hall, past the empty rooms, all the way into ...

Riley!

She was running through the halls as well. But bumping into Bryce stopped her in her tracks.

"You!" she shouted.

"Me!" Bryce shouted back.

"We were in the Screamin' Beagles together! Remember that?" she said. "You wore a Skittle costume. And I ate your fish stick!"

Bryce did remember, because that happened less than a month ago. And he recognized this Riley from the Screamin' Beagles universe because she was still wearing the same Ping-Pong ball costume.

But he was also confused. "I thought we talked about this already," he said. "You told me all about your adventures."

"No, I didn't, because I'm having my adventures RIGHT NOW," Riley said. "Wait. Maybe that means you met *future* me? In the past? Is that possible?"

"Well, I guess the past and the future can sorta be the same thing," Bryce said as he scratched at his head. "Because technically every single day is called *today*. And every *tomorrow* becomes a *today*. And every *today* becomes a *yesterday*. Which means every day is a yesterday, a today, *and* a tomorrow, and that means that . . . wait, I'm confused."

"So am I," Riley said. "But I think it means that I do make it back to my original universe in the end, doesn't it? And at the exact same moment that I left. How entirely four-dimensional of me."

"Four-dimensional?" Bryce asked, because Bryce hadn't read Chapter Twenty-Four of this book. But you have, so you'll understand what Riley said next.

"If I ended up back where I started, then it means that not only can I travel to different universes. I can also travel to different times, across all four dimensions. Holy vegetarian lasagna, that's cool. Gotta love those fish sticks!"

Bryce looked down at her hand. It was empty.

"But where's your fish stick?" he asked.

"Stolen," she said. "That monster played a similar trick on me."

"You mean the Rainbow Specter?"

"I've been calling him Stealy O'Stupidface, but Rainbow Specter works, too."

"Do you know where it went?" Bryce asked.

"I sure do," she said as she grabbed Bryce's hand. "Follow me."

Then she led him down the hall to the gym. When she opened the doors, they were confronted by countless fish sticks piled on the gym floor. The fish sticks formed a mountain in the middle of the gym. Atop that mountain, with its colorful skin undulating, was the Rainbow Specter. It didn't seem to notice them.

"The monster took over the school before I got here," Riley whispered. "And it's been grabbing all the fish sticks it can, though I'm not sure why."

"Maybe it has a laser nose," Bryce whispered back.

Riley's eyes narrowed "That's a . . . possibility. The reason doesn't really matter. All that matters is that it stole *our* fish sticks and if we want to get out of here, we have to get them back."

"But there are so many fish sticks," Bryce said. "How will we know which ones are ours?"

"Well, mine is already half-eaten, so that helps. What about yours?"

"I haven't even licked this one yet."

"Well, then you're gonna have to start licking as many as possible."

"Licking as many as possible? Like . . . with my tongue?"

"I know. Sounds amazing, right? But

there's a problem. If you try to touch any of them, the monster will come after you. I haven't been able to distract it at all. Maybe you have an idea?"

Bryce thought for a moment. He hadn't thought about distractions since Vice Principal Meehan had accused him of being one. But back then, distractions were considered a bad thing, something to hide away in the drab plastic container at the back of his brain. But now . . .

"I have an idea," Bryce said. "A good one."

"O-kay?" Riley said, waiting for him to elaborate.

"Okay," Bryce replied, not elaborating.

"Well, come on, tell me your good idea," Riley said. But she said it so loud that the Rainbow Specter finally heard them. It turned its fiery eyes toward them.

"Oh yeah," Bryce whispered. "That'd be helpful, huh? It's simple. We just have to make it fall in love."

"Oh . . . yeah . . . simple."

"Of course, we're gonna need to sneak into the equipment room," Bryce whispered. "Which is on the other side of Mount Fishy."

"The equipment room? To make it fall in love?"

"Obviously. But how are we going to get there?"

Riley looked up at the ceiling as she patted a hand on her Ping-Pong ball costume, and she said, "Now *I* have an idea."

Chapter Twenty-Nine

THE LOVE SONG OF THE RAINBOW SPECTER

A few minutes later, Bryce and Riley were crawling through the heating ducts, climbing above the gym toward the equipment room.

"Just so you know, this was not the best idea and I would not recommend this idea, especially to impressionable children," Riley said. "It's very dangerous."

"Agreed," Bryce said, as he peered

through a vent. "But we don't have to do it for much longer, because I think we're here."

They soon had the vent open and were climbing down into the dark equipment room. After Bryce tripped over a Hula-Hoop and Riley crashed into a pommel horse, they found the light switch and lit up the room.

"There," Bryce said, pointing to a rainbow-colored mound in the corner. "I'm so glad it exists in this universe, too."

It was the giant parachute that the gym teacher, Mr. Trundle, brought out on parachute days.

Riley was starting to figure things out. "Oh. Okay."

"Remember the lyrics to 'Weird New Place'?"

"Of course. It's the Screamin' Beagles' best song."

"Okay, let's do this," Bryce said, as he lifted the rainbow parachute over their heads, like a sheet over a ghost.

Bryce and Riley both stayed hidden beneath the parachute when they exited the equipment room and entered the gym. The Rainbow Specter didn't see them at first. But it certainly heard them. Because they were singing the last verse to "Weird New Place" as loud as they could.

I don't need to go out and roam,
I don't even need to leave my home,
Right now we can end this chase
If you join me in this weird new place.

Upon hearing the singing, the Rainbow Specter turned, and it made a sound. Not a human sound, but it was a happy sound nonetheless. Bryce thought it sounded like a dolphin playing a didgeridoo, if you can imagine such a thing. (And if you can, please tell us what that sounds like, because we can't imagine it.)

The Rainbow Specter floated down from the mountain toward them, undulating and making that inhuman and happy sound. It was so loud that it caused a disturbance in Mount Fishy.

There was a rumble.

There was a quake.

And Riley could sense what was happening.

She grabbed Bryce by the wrist

and pulled him to the door. The whole mountain collapsed with a thunderous boom as they rushed into the hall. But this didn't slow the Rainbow Specter. It was still hot on their heels.

"Just keep singing!" Bryce shouted as they sped up.

They had poked a few holes in the parachute so they could see out, and together they ran toward the Dungeon, singing the chorus.

Weird new place
Weirder than outer space . . .

Chapter Thirty

INTERDIMENSIONAL

"The Dungeon isn't secure," Riley said as they bumbled down the stairs, trying to see through the eye holes. "That's where the Rainbow Specter first ambushed me. We can't lock it in there."

"We're not locking it in there," Bryce said. "If the Dungeon is like the Dungeon in my universe, then it's interdimensional."

"How so?"

"You'll see. I hope."

When they broke through the door, she did see. The answer was written in graffiti on one of the toilet stalls.

"Oh, right!" she exclaimed. "Okay, let's get in the stall. It'll be here soon."

They scrambled into a toilet stall and climbed up the back, pressing their bodies against the wall. They started singing again to coax the lovesick Rainbow Specter inside.

Weird new place!

Makin' my bloodstream race!

Almost immediately, the Rainbow Specter appeared in the doorway of the stall, emitting that strange sound. It inched closer to them.

Bryce slipped a hand out from under

the parachute and grabbed the top edge of the toilet stall. Riley did the same thing.

Weird new place!

Puts me in a state of grace!

The Rainbow Specter started to climb onto the toilet bowl, and the strange sound became faster and more excited. Bryce and Riley pressed their bodies flat against the wall, so that it couldn't touch them. And Bryce eased his foot toward the toilet handle, as they sang the last line of the song.

Ain't nowhere else I'd rather be than a . . .

He pushed down on the handle with his foot, and as the toilet started to flush, they shouted the final words.

Weird! New! Place!

The flushing got more intense. The toilet roared and the Rainbow Specter screamed, which sounded like a hyena playing the bagpipes.

It had a good reason to scream. Because it was being sucked into the toilet!

So too was the rainbow parachute. And Bryce and Riley would've been sucked in as well, if they hadn't been holding so tightly onto the stall. The suction was even more powerful than the tuxedoed tornadoes.

But after a few seconds, the flushing stopped.

Everything was quiet and still.

And the Rainbow Specter and the rainbow parachute were both gone.

Bryce and Riley didn't say a word. They simply climbed down off the toilet tank, stepped out and stood next to the sinks. They turned to the stall and both marveled at the graffiti.

Flush The Toilet + U Will B Sucked into the Burrito Dimension!

"Hope the Rainbow Specter likes wearing tortilla underpants as much as it likes stealing fish sticks," Bryce said.

"And I hope you like licking fish sticks as much as I do," Riley said. "Because it's time to start licking fish sticks, my friend."

Chapter Thirty-One

THE GREAT FISH STICK LICK

And that's exactly what happened. Fish stick licking.

Bryce and Riley returned to the cafetorium, opened the door, confronted a solid wall of fish sticks and devised a plan.

Bryce would lick a fish stick and when it didn't send him to another universe, he would hand it to Riley. If Riley was hungry, she would eat it. If not, she would place it in a cooler so she could eat it later.

Gross? Yes. Wasteful? No.

Lick, Pass, Chomp. Lick, Pass, Chomp. Lick, Pass, Save.

You get the idea.

If Bryce found a half-eaten fish stick in the mix (there were only a few of those), Riley would lick it and see if it was her fish stick.

This kept them busy for over three weeks. Bryce spent twelve hours a day licking fish sticks, at an average rate of one fish stick every two seconds. At night they slept on gym mats in the equipment closet.

Of course, they had plenty of time to talk. And both of them liked to talk. Riley told Bryce about her universe and her adventures beyond it. He told her about his universe and how he ended up in this particular universe.

"It's strange," Riley commented at one point. "Why were you wearing the Skittle costume again?"

"Because it was Halloween in my universe, and I wanted to express myself," Bryce said.

"But gummy bears are your favorite candy, right? Skittles, on the other hand, are Keisha's favorite candy. I wonder what that means?"

"Huh," Bryce said, because he hadn't thought that through entirely.

"Are you friends with Keisha in your universe?"

"Sorta. Or not really. I mean, I know her. I . . . *want* to be her friend. But the only things she talks to me about are homework . . . and Locker 37."

"I see. Do you think that's why you dressed as a Skittle? For her attention?"

"I'm not sure."

"And do you think her attention is worth you getting in trouble with your vice principal?"

"I don't know."

"And what about wearing costumes on Halloween? Is that something that's still important to you?"

"I can't say."

"Well, then I guess you have a lot to think about until you find your fish stick," Riley told him.

"I guess so," Bryce replied.

And so Bryce thought. And licked. And thought. He did this for a while, in silence, as Riley either ate or stored the non-interdimensional fish sticks in her cooler.

Bryce considered his original list of conditions for an ideal universe. It had grown to six conditions, but he eventually revised it and settled on that single last condition: *Must Feel Right.* It was starting to become clear that it was the only thing that mattered.

Bryce thought about costumes. And vice principals. And himself. He thought about friends and school and music. He thought about Keisha, and the different versions of her he had met, and how they were all familiar, but none of them felt like the true Keisha. He went through his basket of weird thoughts, and his basket of nice thoughts, and even that drab plastic container full of thoughts he preferred not to think about.

Surprisingly, there were some thoughts about Keisha in that container, too. They weren't bad thoughts. They were about how Bryce liked her more than anyone else at school, in a way he was never fully comfortable with. Until now.

Now he was ready to think about those thoughts. And he thought about them and thought and thought and then ...

He picked up a fish stick that looked a little different from the rest.

It was a little battered (pun intended). It had what appeared to be monkey fur on it. Also cartoon rabbit fur. It was, quite frankly, disgusting. But Bryce had the impulse to eat the whole darn thing in one bite. So that's what he did.

Gulp.

The world went blurry. But this time it was a different, interdimensional blurry, where all the universes Bryce had visited folded in on themselves and flashed before his eyes in an instant.

Chapter Thirty-Two

AN UNNECESSARILY LONG CHAPTER ABOUT GEOMETRY . . . AND FISH STICKS

You probably have a lot of questions. Perhaps many of them are related to the burrito dimension. Now is neither the time nor the place to answer them, mainly because the publisher said this book can't exceed a certain page count or else it will cost too much. That's a real bummer, because there's a very good story we'd love to share about a young

Sammy Rao, an interdimensional Riley, and a Sharpie.

Oh well. At least we can answer a far more important question. And that question is this: Exactly how many fish sticks did Bryce have to lick?

The answer: About one out of every eleven fish sticks in the cafetorium.

And how many fish sticks is that?

To figure that out, it helps to know how to calculate the volume of three-dimensional objects.

And how would someone know that?

Well, by going to school and paying attention, and—

You know what? Just listen.

In most universes, a calculation like this

wouldn't be exact. Because in most universes fish sticks do not stack perfectly like a series of bricks lined end-to-end. But the universe of the Rainbow Specter was not most universes. The fish sticks *did* stack perfectly there. When Mount Fishy crumbled, all the fish sticks lined up, side-to-side, end-to-end, and top-to-bottom. There were no cracks or open spaces between them. It was as if the cafetorium became instantly paved with a solid layer of fish sticks.

That's helpful for us, because we can figure out exactly how many fish sticks were in the cafetorium, using the formula for volume of a rectangular prism. Volume is a fancy way of saying how much stuff fits inside other stuff. And a rectangular prism is a fancy way of saying a cube or box with rectangular sides.

Okay, let's start with the cafetorium. If you've ever looked at the blueprints of Hopewell Elementary (we have), then you know the cafetorium was 50 feet long and 40 feet wide. Multiply those two numbers to get the area of the floor, which is 2,000 square feet.

What is a square foot?

Well, simply picture a floor tile that is 1 foot long and 1 foot wide. Or better yet, picture the sleeve for an album. You know, the cover for a record? An LP? The vinyl discs you spin on a turntable for analog music at its scratchy best?

1 foot length x 1 foot width

Before your time, huh? Okay, fine. Go back to the floor tile.

Now picture 2,000 of those tiles covering the floor.

Of course, measuring area and square feet only helps for two-dimensional things. We need to take this equation all the way to the . . . third dimension! That's right. We must add height to figure out the volume. Because volume equals LENGTH times WIDTH times HEIGHT.

 Length x Width x Height

The stack of fish sticks reached 3 feet from the ground. So if we multiply those 3 feet by the 2,000 square feet, we get 6,000 cubic feet. Cubic feet are like square feet, but they're measured in cubes that are 1 foot long, 1 foot high, and 1 foot wide.

Think of a cardboard box with 12-inch sides

(after all, there are 12 inches in 1 foot). Or maybe think of a milk crate. You know, the type that milkmen use when they deliver milk to your doorstep? You know, the milk in the glass bottles with cream on top and . . .

Each side is 12 inches

Not ringing a bell? Jeez. We get it. You're young and cool and don't care about the history of the mid-twentieth-century dairy industry. It's quite alright. We're not offended. We'll just stick with the boring old cardboard box and inform you that 6,000 of those boring old boxes is the volume we need to completely fill the bottom three feet of the cafetorium.

Now, to figure out how many fish sticks will fit in 6,000 cubic feet, we next have to figure out the volume of the fish sticks, or how many cubic feet each fish stick takes up. So we will multiply their length (4 inches), their width (1 inch), and their height/thickness (1/2 inch). That gives us 2 cubic . . .

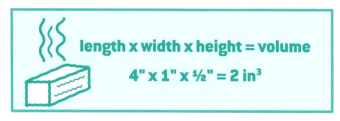

length x width x height = volume

$$4" \times 1" \times \frac{1}{2}" = 2 \text{ in}^3$$

Inches. Not surprisingly, a cubic inch is a lot smaller than a cubic foot. In fact, there are 1,728 cubic inches (or 12 inches LONG times 12 inches WIDE times 12 inches HIGH) in just 1 cubic foot!

So if we divide 1,728 cubic inches by 2 cubic inches, we get 864. That's the number of fish sticks that would fit in a cubic foot (or a milk crate). Multiply those 864 fish sticks by the 6,000 cubic feet we need to fill the bottom 3 feet of the cafetorium and we get . . .

5,184,000 fish sticks!

Of course, that number represents the maximum number of fish sticks Bryce would've had to lick if we assumed that the last fish stick he licked was the one he was looking for. (Say that ten times fast.)

But, Bryce didn't have to lick that many. As we mentioned earlier, he only had to lick one out of every eleven fish sticks in the cafetorium. And if you remember the previous chapter, you'll remember he was licking a fish stick every two seconds, for twelve hours a day, for over three weeks. That means, if we use the following formula:

> **60 seconds per minute, times** . . .
>
> **60 minutes per hour, times** . . .
>
> **12 hours per day, times** . . .
>
> **7 days per week, times** . . .
>
> **3 weeks, divided by** . . .
>
> **2 seconds per lick, we get** . . .
>
> **453,600 fish sticks licked!**

And you'll notice if we divide the total 5,184,000 fish sticks in the cafetorium by 453,600 fish sticks licked, we get . . .

One out of 11.4285714286 fish sticks in the cafetorium licked.

This is all a very exhausting way of saying that Bryce was both very lucky and very unlucky at the same time. And he brought that lucky/unlucky feeling with him all the way across all ten dimensions to . . .

Chapter Thirty-Three
HOPEWELL ELEMENTARY

Bryce was alone and he was standing next to Locker 37. It was empty. His hand was empty, too.

He was dressed in the clothes he had been wearing while licking the fish sticks, which were a sweatshirt and jeans (with shorts underneath, in case the weather warmed up). The Skittle costume, and the green face paint were long gone.

Which was a great relief to Vice Principal Meehan, who was now standing at the end of the hall.

"Thank you for removing the costume, son," Vice Principal Meehan said as he approached. "You look much less distracting now."

The hall looked like the hall from Bryce's home universe. And Vice Principal Meehan looked like the Vice Principal Meehan that Bryce knew. Everything seemed . . . familiar.

"Is it still . . . Halloween?" Bryce asked.

"Unless something changed in the last ten minutes, it sure is," Vice Principal Meehan said. "Thank you again for removing the costume. Enjoy wearing it again outside of school hours, Mr. Dodd."

It was a harmless enough thing for Vice Principal Meehan to say, but it made Bryce angry. And Bryce never got angry. He certainly had reason to be, though. He had gone through so much. He had worked and suffered and faced unspeakable dangers. And now that he was no longer wearing his costume, it all felt like a big waste.

That's why Bryce hardly even thought about what he said next. The words simply spilled out of his mouth.

"I *will* enjoy it," he said. "I will indeed. And I'll enjoy it when I wear another costume to school. That's right. I'll be wearing costumes again. You don't know when it'll happen, but it'll happen, Vice Principal Meehan. Believe me. I will wear another costume to school. And I will face the consequences. Because it might be a distraction, but distractions can sometimes be a good thing. Especially in tough times when kids need distractions in their lives."

"You are—" Vice Principal Meehan started to say, but Bryce interrupted him.

"I am Bryce Dodd, sir. And I have faced laser noses and monkeys and tornadoes. And I have licked almost half a million fish sticks. And I am weird, but I am nice, and I will express myself in ways that make me feel weird and nice. And I don't care what happens to me anymore, or what people think of me. Even if they bully me or punish me or decide not to be my friend. I'm ready to face those things. Because this is who I am. And who I will always be."

Vice Principal Meehan stared at him for a moment.

In the past, this might have made Bryce uncomfortable. But remember, he had completely opened that drab container in his brain, the one where he kept the things that he preferred not to think about. He was finally ready to admit that those things, as difficult as they might've been to confront, were a part of his life. He couldn't deny them any longer. He was willing to face any consequences anyone could dish out. It was worth it to him.

But there were no consequences. Vice

Principal Meehan simply nodded and said, "Duly noted, Mr. Dodd. But we shall talk about that on a later date. For now, Happy Halloween."

Before Bryce could say anything else, Vice Principal Meehan turned and walked away. Bryce wasn't sure he had anything more to say anyway. He was feeling a bit overwhelmed. He had spent nearly two months traveling through different universes, only to end up back on Halloween.

Did that mean this was a universe where every day was Halloween? Or was this, could this possibly be . . .

Home?

There was only one way to find out.

Chapter Thirty-Four

KEISHA

Bryce walked through the school, observing everything he could. Again, it all had a familiar feeling about it. The posters, the color of paint on the walls, the fellow students, all rushing to class. A clock near the main entrance told him it was time for first period, and there was a calendar on the glass door to the front office that confirmed it was October 31.

Halloween. And no one was wearing costumes. Interesting.

Bryce rushed to his first period class. On October 31 in his own universe, that class was music, so that's where he went. When he entered the music room, he was greeted by Mr. Gregson.

"Good morning, Bryce," he said. "Happy Halloween."

He noticed Riley and Carson chatting near the piano. Hunter was rummaging through the percussion instruments. And Keisha was in the center of the room, waiting patiently and quietly for class to start.

When Bryce spotted her, he remembered all the versions of Keisha he had met on his adventures. And he remembered how every time he met one, he felt nervous, like he couldn't talk to her or say something to her. It wasn't that he was afraid of Keisha. It was simply that he liked her. A lot. And he was never sure how to tell her that.

Until now. Bryce took a deep breath and approached this version of Keisha, saying, "Happy Halloween."

"Happy Halloween," Keisha replied as he got closer. "Looks like you had to take off that costume you were wearing this morning on the bus, huh? I could've told you that was a bad idea. Very foolish. Still, it was kinda brave."

There was something about Keisha's combination of friendliness, confidence, and brutal honesty. It was giving Bryce an ever stronger, more familiar feeling about this universe.

"Yeah," he said to her. "Vice Principal Meehan wanted me to take it off, but I sort of lost it along the way."

"Along the way to music class?" she said. "That's odd."

"You have no idea," Bryce said.

He wanted to ask her what she thought about his costume. He wanted to tell her what he'd gone through. He wanted to say so many things to her, but Mr. Gregson started to talk before Bryce could say anything else.

"Today, friends, in honor of Halloween, we're going to sing one of my favorite songs," Mr. Gregson said. "It's called 'Werewolves of London'."

Keisha nudged Bryce with her elbow, and asked, "Is that a Screamin' Beagles song? Those weirdos are your favorite band, right?"

Bryce smiled. It wasn't technically a Screamin' Beagles song, but that didn't matter. All that mattered was that Keisha was still talking to him.

"Yeah, they're my favorite weirdos and my favorite band," Bryce said. "This isn't one of their original songs, but they sometimes do a cover version of it."

"Cover versions are rarely as good as the original, don't you think?" Keisha said.

"I guess it sometimes depends on your point of view."

"How do you mean?"

"It depends on which one you're most

familiar with," Bryce said.

"That's a good point," Keisha said with a nod.

Mr. Gregson sat down at the piano. He was about to start playing, and so Bryce realized he couldn't talk to Keisha for much longer. But he felt that he had to get a few more words in. "I know we're not technically friends—" he started to say.

But Keisha cut him off, asking, "And why do you think that?"

"Well . . . I guess I don't know that for sure," Bryce said with a shrug.

"I know something for sure," Keisha said as she put a hand on his shoulder. "You're weird. But you're nice. And from my point of view, that makes you about as good a friend as a kid can have."

The words gave Bryce more courage than ever before. He was so glad he had finally decided to talk to her about how he felt, and he was ready to tell her more of his feelings, but she stopped him by putting a finger to her lips.

Then Keisha reached down into her backpack and pulled out a package of Skittles. She slipped it into his hand and smiled, like this was a little secret

between two very good friends.

As Bryce pocketed the candy, he marveled at this version of Keisha. He was now almost certain she was the version of Keisha he was most familiar with.

Meanwhile, Mr. Gregson, who was also known as Greg Greg, started to play the piano. And that's when Bryce started to howl like a werewolf.

Chapter Thirty-Five

WHAT DOES IT MEAN TO YOU?

When class was over, Keisha hurried off to social studies, but Bryce lingered behind.

"Can I talk to you for a moment?" he asked Mr. Gregson.

"Sure," Mr. Gregson replied as he put away all the percussion instruments Hunter had left strewn on the floor.

"Class was really fun today," he said.

"That song was really fun. But do you mind if I ask you about another song? About a song you wrote?"

"I don't mind at all," Mr. Gregson said.

"My favorite Screamin' Beagles' song is 'Weird New Place.' But I'm not sure I really understand it. I was wondering where that weird new place is."

"You mean geographically?"

"Maybe. Or, you know . . . interdimensionally?"

Mr. Gregson smiled at that thought. And then he said, "Some people think that song is about a girl and a strange and wonderful vacation. But to me, the song isn't about an actual location you can go to. Or even about an actual girl. It's a love song. But it's a love song about music. It's about how music takes my soul to a weird new place. It doesn't matter where I am. Music sweeps me away."

"Oh," Bryce said. "That makes sense."

"That's only what it means to me, though," Mr. Gregson said. "It could mean something entirely different to you. So let me ask you this. What does it mean to you?"

It was at that moment that Bryce was finally sure of something. He was home. This universe felt even better than the universe with Locker 37,000. It felt more than familiar. It felt right.

But there *was* something different about it. His brain. It had changed. It was like those three separate parts didn't exist anymore. The weird and nice

and uncomfortable were now all mixed
together. Which made his mind feel like
it was in a weird new place. And he liked
that weird new place.

"It means we all have the potential to go to a weird new place," Bryce said. "And the power to go there is inside of each of us. We just have to find it and be open to it."

Mr. Gregson smiled and nodded. "I dig that, Bryce. I dig that a lot."

Bryce smiled back and said, "Don't dig too far, Mr. Gregson, or you might end up in some upside-down world where the letter A is the letter Z and wombat poop is round. You know what I mean?"

Mr. Gregson had no idea what he meant, but he nodded anyway and said, "Thanks for the advice."

Bryce flashed him a thumbs-up in response, but he knew he couldn't hang around for much longer. Because his mind's weird new place was inspiring him to do something.

He pulled a piece of paper and a pencil out of his backpack. He thanked Mr. Gregson one last time. Then he rushed out of the room.

But Bryce didn't go to social studies. He went directly to Locker 37.

Chapter Thirty-Six
THIS CHAPTER IS ABOUT YOU

Locker 37 was empty. But that was okay. That's what Bryce wanted. Because he wasn't going to take something from the locker. He was going to leave something inside it.

He had just scribbled out a letter and he placed it inside the locker. Then he closed the locker and hurried off to social studies.

And what did the letter say?

Well, if you are a master of all ten dimensions (as we assume you are), then you already know. But we'll print it here anyway. Why? Just because.

Hey there,

It's me, Bryce! How are you doing? I'm guessing you can't really answer that because this is just a letter. I'm also guessing you're not doing too great. I mean, why else would you be looking in Locker 37?

I'm sorry that you're in a pickle. And I'm sorry that I already used the one magical thingy that Locker 37 was giving out today. If it makes you feel any better, I had to lick half a million fish sticks after I opened Locker 37. So, unless you're Riley, you're probably glad you didn't have to go through all that.

But you probably still want some help. You can always stop me in the hall and ask me for help. I'm here and I'm happy to do what I can. But if there's nothing I can do, maybe there's something I can say. Let's start with the truth. Which is this:

You are smart and brave and kind and you can do things and be things you never imagined you could do or be. Because you are bigger than your problems. It might not seem like that right now, but it's true. I started the morning trying to ignore my problems and then I spent a VERY LONG TIME trying to run away from those problems. Neither worked. You see, what I really had to do was face my problems.

That's the most important thing Locker 37 taught me. There are an infinite number of universes and an infinite number of people who could exist in them. What could exist doesn't matter, though. What matters is that of all the people who could exist, you are one who actually does exist.

That's pretty much magic. Which

means you're pretty much magic. You really are. Maybe even more magic than this silly locker. (Sorry to say that about you, Locker 37, but even you have to admit you're pretty silly.)

I guess the main thing I'm trying to tell you is this:

Leave the letter here.

Close the locker door.

Face your problem and do what I know you can do.

You've got this!

Your pal,

Bryce

P.S. If you find out that you don't actually *got* this, that's okay, too. Just try opening Locker 37 tomorrow. I bet you'll find a rocket backpack that'll help you fly, or some cargo pants that'll give you the ability to cook really good chimichangas, or something else cool like that. Until then . . . see you in class!